What A Trip!

"Gee," Mel said. "I don't think I'm in New Jersey anymore."

Mel took a look around. The bushes and the trees and the houses seemed the same . . . But wait!

Everything was pointy! There was a dog with a pointy head.
There were pointy birds and pointy clouds and pointy cars.
It was a pointy dimension. "Wow!" said Mel.

Mel raced down the block to see what else he could see and just as he rounded the corner, he tripped and fell right out of the pointy dimension.

"Ma, Dad!" Mel shouted. "I just came from another dimension! I discovered another dimension!"

"Mel, you look pale, have some fruit," Marsha, Mel's mother, suggested.

"Oh, Ma!"

Manny, Mel's father, also had advice. "Mel, do something useful. Go wash the car."

"But I was there!" Mel insisted. "I was there!"

The next day, Mel told all his friends about his amazing discovery. He drew diagrams. He made charts. He described every detail. But did anyone believe him? No.

Instead, they laughed at him and made fun of him. So, after a while, Mel tried to forget about the pointy dimension.

But he couldn't. He couldn't get it out of his mind.

All he thought about was pointy things. At school, he sharpened pencils. For dinner, he asked for swordfish.

Mel even went back to Tottenhotten Street and tried to trip himself.

He tripped and he tripped, trying to get back to the other dimension.

"The boy's a nut!" Mel's father said.

"Maybe he should see a doctor," Mel's mother said.

His parents were worried.

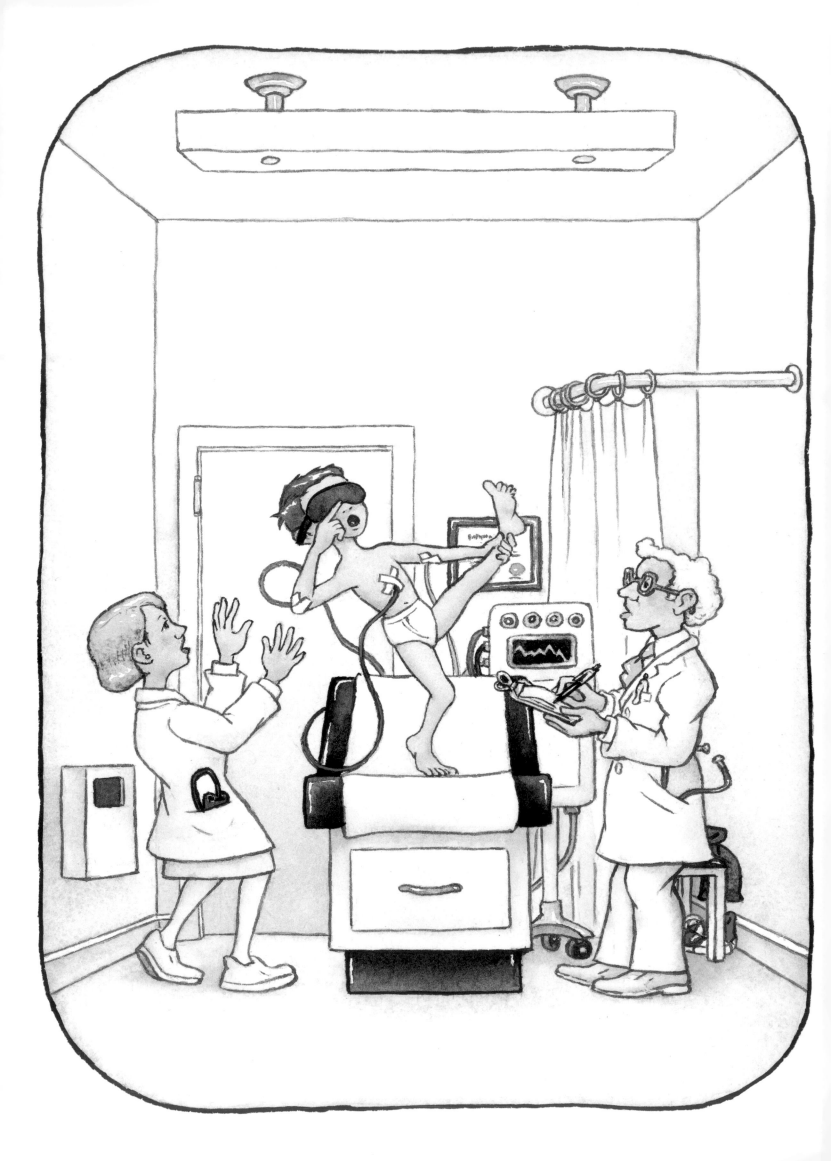

So Mel went to the doctor.

After several exhaustive and comprehensive tests, the doctor finally offered his diagnosis:

"The boy's a klutz."

Mel, for his own good, was sent to Camp Stymie, a specialty camp for klutzes. Still, Mel never stopped believing in the pointy dimension. Day and night, he collected arrowheads. In arts and crafts, he made spears.

Within a week, Mel was sent home.

"That's it, Mel," his father announced. "You're coming to work with me. Maybe that will straighten you out."

In the morning, Mel went to his father's work. Manny was the manager of the largest garbage dump in the state of New Jersey.

"Just think, Mel," his father said proudly, "when you grow up, your life can be garbage, just like mine."

Mel shrugged. Then, as he tried to lift a couple of garbage bags, he tripped and fell into the other dimension.
Uh-oh!

His father was stunned.

Mel's mother was hysterical. "Manny!" she cried. "You lost our son in the dump? How could you!"

"Well," Mel's father explained, "one minute he was there and the next minute he was gone."

"Oh, where's my Melville?" Marsha shrieked. "Where's my Melville!"

"I'm right here!" he called out. "I'm in the other dimension!" Mel had ended up in the living room of his pointy, other-dimension house.

"Mel! Your mother is plotzing," his father said as he checked under the couch. "Stop this nonsense and come out here this minute."

"But it's true!" Mel said. "I'm in our pointy-dimension house. There's our TV. There's our piano. There's . . . Ma, there's you!"

Coming out of the pointy kitchen was Mel's mother. A pointy mother!

"Mel!" his pointy mother gasped. "What in the begeebees happened to you? Manny! *Manny!*" A pointy Manny rushed into the room.

"You *see*, Marsha," Mel's pointy father said, "you spoil him and look what happens. He's round!"

"No, no, I'm—" Mel started to say when in walked another . . . Mel!

Pointy Mel!

Pointy Marsha fainted.

"It's a monster!" pointy Mel screamed, pointing at unpointy Mel.

"There's a monster in the house, there's a monster in the house!"

"I'm not a monster!" said unpointy Mel. "I'm Mel—from New Jersey!"

"You're not Mel!" pointy Marsha proclaimed. "You're an imposter!"
She grabbed a pointy rolling pin.

"But I *am* Mel!" Mel cried. "Ma, Dad! Help! I'm stuck in the pointy
dimension!"

The whole pointy family chased unpointy Mel around the pointy living room as he ran for his life!

But luckily Mel tripped on the carpeting his father, in both dimensions, never fixed—and fell straight out of the other dimension.

"Oh, Melville!" unpointy Marsha gushed as she gave her unpointy Mel a huge hug.

"Welcome home, son," said unpointy Manny.

From that day on, Mel's parents never doubted him again. Even when Mel told them he'd just come back from the lost island of Atlantis, they kissed him and said, "Mel, Mel, you're such a smarty."

Yes. Melville.

What a trip!